This book belongs to:

....

....

Quarto is the authority on a wide range of topics.

Quarto educates, entertains and enriches the lives of our readers—enthusiasts and lovers of hands-on living.

www.quartoknows.com

Editor: Tasha Percy
Designer: Krina Patel
Editorial Director: Victoria Garrard
Art Director: Laura Roberts-Jensen

First published in the UK in 2015 by QED Publishing
Part of The Quarto Group, The Old Brewery, 6 Blundell Street, London, N7 9BH

A catalogue record for this book is available from the British Library.

ISBN 978 1 78171 691 5

Manufactured in Guangdong, China TT092017

9 8 7 6 5 4 3 2

When I Grow Up...

QED

Fergus was having his morning wash.

"What should I be when I grow up?" he asked.

Mum thought for a moment,
and then said with a smile,

"You should be **clean**. Now hold still..."

"Hmm," Fergus thought. "Is that all?"
He went to find his brothers and sisters.

"What should I be when
I grow up?" he asked them.

"Playful!" laughed the puppies, as they chased each other in the sunshine.

While out walking, he bumped
into Buster standing by his gate.

"Buster, what do **you** think
I should be when I grow up?"

"HELPFUL," barked Buster, as he chased a cat off his fence.

"A dog should be helpful, playful, oh, and clean," thought Fergus.

At the park Fergus spotted Penelope.

"Hello Penelope. What do you think I should be when I grow up?"

"Lovely to see you Fergus. I'd have to say *charming*," replied Penelope, and went on her way.

"A dog should be charming, helpful, playful and clean," thought Fergus to himself.

Just then, Bolt **ZOOMED** past, chasing rabbits.

"What do you think
I should be when
I grow up, Bolt?"

"QUICK" he panted, as the rabbit disappeared down its burrow.

"A dog should be quick, charming, helpful, playful and clean," thought Fergus.

Fergus was on his way home when he
saw Maggie sitting by the farm gate.

"Hello Maggie. What should I be
when I grow up?" he asked her.

"OBEDIENT," she said, as she dashed off to the call of the farmer's whistle.

"So," thought Fergus, "a dog should be...

...OBEDIENT...

...QUICK...

...charming...

HELPFUL...

 **...Playful...**

...and *clean.*"

When he was nearly home Fergus
was greeted by his friend Jester.

"Hello Jester, I've been trying to work out what
I should be when I grow up. What do you think?"

"**Friendly!**" said Jester,

and they wagged
their tails at each other.

Mum was waiting for Fergus.
"You look a little **worried**,
Fergus. What is the matter?"

"I asked everyone what I should be when I grow up,"
he said, "and they all gave me different answers."

"I have to be **friendly**, OBEDIENT, *QUICK*, charming, **HELPFUL**, Playful... and **clean!**

Can a dog really be all those things at once?"

"That is rather a lot for one small dog," she said. "But there's only one thing you really need to be – *loved!*"

NEXT STEPS

Ask the children if they can remember how many dogs Fergus met on his walk? What did the dogs say Fergus should be?

Dogs come in all shapes and sizes, and can be long haired or short haired. Do the children know any types of dog other than the ones in the story?

Get the children to guess what is the biggest breed of dog? Which is the smallest? What else can they find out about dogs?

Ask the children if they had a dog what kind would they choose? What would they call it?

Get the children to draw their ideal dog and give it a name. Ask if they would rather have another kind of pet?

Some people say a dog is a man's best friend. What do the children think makes a good friend? What words would they use to describe what makes their best friends special.

Some dogs have jobs, like Maggie the sheepdog in the story. Do the children know any other jobs a dog might do?

Ask the children if they know what they want to be when they grow up?